BAD NEWS

"I'm telling you guys," Jo said as she tugged her baseball cap into place. "After next Saturday, the Slashers are gonna be *history!*"

Dave had been only half listening to his teammates. In the midst of all the high-spirited gloating and glorious predictions, he blurted out, "Mr. Bowman's sick, isn't he, Jim?"

Jim wet his lips. "I've been holding off for the right time to tell you guys," Jim answered, without taking his eyes off the road. "You're right, Dave. Mr. Bowman's had a heart attack. He's in the hospital right now."

A moment earlier the Bullsmobile had been filled with confident yapping and laughter—the sounds of victory. Now there was total silence.

Dave, in a panic, tried to calm himself by taking a deep breath. But he couldn't do it. He felt as though the wind had been knocked out of him.

Don't miss any of the books in

—a slammin', jammin', in-your-face action series,
new from Bantam Books!

#1 Crashing the Boards

#2 In Your Face!

#3 Trash Talk

#4 Monster Jam

#5 One on One

Coming soon:
#7 Slam Dunk!

SHOW TIME!

by
Hank Herman

BANTAM BOOKS
NEW YORK • TORONTO • LONDON • SYDNEY • AUCKLAND

To Carol, mother of champions

RL 2.6, 007-010

SHOW TIME!
A Bantam Book / July 1996

Produced by Daniel Weiss Associates, Inc.
33 West 17th Street
New York, NY 10011

Cover art by Jeff Mangiat

ISBN: 0-553-48278-5
Published simultaneously in the United States and Canada

Bantam Books are published by Bantam Books, a division of Bantam
Doubleday Dell Publishing Group, Inc. Its trademark, consisting of the
words "Bantam Books" and the portrayal of a rooster, is Registered in U.S.
Patent and Trademark Office and in other countries. Marca Registrada.
Bantam Books, 1540 Broadway, New York, New York 10036.

PRINTED IN THE UNITED STATES OF AMERICA

OPM   0 9 8 7 6 5 4 3 2

CHAPTER 1

"Still going," Dave said, using the words from the popular TV commercial, as he watched the basketball spinning on his right index finger. Every few seconds he had to toss his long blond hair out of his eyes so he could get a good look at the ball.

"But getting a little wobbly," Jo taunted. "Now take a look over here. Mine'll still be spinning when you're in a rocking chair on the porch of an old-age home, dreaming

about your glory days on the Branford Bulls."

Dave stole a nervous glance over at Jo Meyerson, the cocky girl who called herself Dime. ("Because I'm ten times better than Penny Hardaway," she said.) Her brown ponytail was peeking out from under her green baseball cap, which she wore backward. Even though Jo had been a member of the Bulls for most of the summer, Dave was still amazed that a girl could handle the ball the way she could.

What she'd said was true: His ball had started to waver, while the ball on Jo's finger kept going . . . and going . . . and *going*.

"That's just great, Danzig!" Dave heard an angry voice boom at him. "We're supposed to be working on our zone press, and all you and Dime here can think about are your dumb show-off tricks."

Dave turned around in surprise. The voice belonged to seventeen-year-old Nate Bowman, one of the Bulls' two coaches and the best high-school basketball player in Danville County. Nate's trademarks were his gold stud earring and mammoth, size-thirteen sneakers. He and Jim Hopwood, who also  was a star on the Branford High team, had taken over as the Bulls' coaches when Coach McBain and the McBain twins moved to the West Coast at the beginning of the summer. Nate and Jim usually ran the Bulls' practices as a nice-guy–tough-guy pair, with Nate as the nice guy. He usually wasn't a whole lot more mature than the ten-year-olds he coached. As a matter of fact, just when Jim would be hammering home an important point, Nate would often pick up the ball and go flying to the hoop for one of his monster jams.

Now he's *the one yelling at* me *for showing off?* Dave mused. *Maybe he's just a little uptight about our championship game with the Slash—* He caught himself before he finished his thought. He couldn't assume the Bulls would be playing the Slashers. He could just hear Nate's dad, Mr. Bowman, saying,

"Don't count your chickens before they're hatched!" The roly-poly owner of Bowman's Market, who'd almost been drafted by the Knicks in his younger days, had said that to the boys at least a hundred times.

True, the Bulls still had to beat the Portsmouth Panthers the next day in the semifinals to get to the hated Slashers. But while the Panthers were no push-overs, the Bulls and the Slashers were the top two teams in the league, and a rematch of the previous year's championship final seemed inevitable.

Dave had noticed that Nate and Jim, who never allowed the Bulls to take any opponent too lightly, had them working on their zone press and their fast break. These were weapons that had been designed expressly for use against the Slashers.

Dave could understand why the coaches seemed to be breaking their own no-looking-ahead rule: The Sampton Slashers, the most obnoxious, most trash-talking group of hot dogs you could find in the Danville County Basketball League, were the Bulls' archrivals. The year before, the Slashers had beaten the Bulls in the final—with the help, the Bulls thought, of some "hometown" reffing. The Bulls had gotten a small taste of revenge by beating Sampton in an unofficial grudge match at the beginning of the summer but then had been thumped again by the Slashers in their only regular-season game.

Now, in less than two weeks, it would be payback time.

Fortunately, since their last loss to the Slashers, the Bulls had come away with exciting wins over the Essex Eagles and the Harrison Hornets. Starting center Will Hopwood's sprained wrist was fully healed, and spirits were sky-high. Dave didn't want to screw around with the up-tempo mood, and so he decided not to take the scolding from Nate personally. Nate might be a little hyper, but Dave could deal with it.

He turned his attention back to the court, where the Bulls' starters were working a zone press against the subs. When MJ, a backup forward, received the inbounds pass from Mark Fisher, the short guard with the goggles, Dave flew at MJ, arms waving like a windmill.

"Come on, MJ," he teased. "Cough it up. You know you're gonna do it sooner or later."

MJ—his real name, amazingly, was Michael Jordan—was a skinny black kid of medium height who knew more about the game than anyone on the court, and who dressed like a player and talked like a player. The only trouble was, he wasn't very good at *playing*. Since joining the Bulls, he'd actually been more of a plus as an assistant coach than as a forward.

Dave, who enjoyed talking trash almost as much as he did dribbling behind his back, knew he had MJ trapped. "All right, you clumsy piece of toast, just hand me the ball and get it over with."

But while Dave was busy dissing MJ, he dropped his arms for just a moment. MJ, always alert, saw Chunky between mid-court and the top of the key and managed to hit him with an over-the-head two-hand pass.

"Oh, Da-ave," taunted Chunky. "Yoo-hoo! The ball's over here now. Come and get it!" Chunky Schwartz was on the heavy side and tended to get exhausted before the first time-out. This made him the butt of a lot of friendly joking. He had a good sense of humor and was able to take the ribbing, but he liked dishing it out, too.

Just as Dave was about to start hounding Chunky, he heard Nate bellow, "What exactly is going on here? Why wasn't anyone within a mile of Chunky for that outlet? Hopwood, aren't you supposed to be the rover in this press? What is this, your nap time?"

Dave saw Will Hopwood's face turn bright red. Will, the tall center, was one of the three original Bulls, along with Dave and Brian Simmons. Will took his hoops seriously, and his knowledge of the game—plus his awesome turn-around jumper and his tough rebounding—made him the team leader. His goal was to star for Branford High one day, like his older brother, Jim.

Will didn't take criticism lightly.

"C'mon, Nate, ease up," Jim said.

"Will was double-teaming me, like he's supposed to. Give the subs some credit. Chunky was in the right spot, and MJ made a good pass."

"Good pass, *right*," Nate muttered sarcastically. "Will was sleeping, and Dave, as usual, was blabbing away. It wouldn't kill them to play some hoops for a change."

Jim said nothing further to Nate, but Dave noticed he did give him a sharp look.

Dave found himself wondering if there wasn't more to Nate's nastiness than the pressure of the upcoming rematch with Sampton. The real Nate would have been looking forward to a challenge like that, so his Bulls could strut their stuff. Instead, he was whining like an old lady.

Jim told the Bulls to take a break and grab some water. Jim usually called for a water break when he needed a chance to think about what to do next, or when things were getting a little too tense—the way they were right then.

In a few minutes they returned to

the blacktop. "All right, you guys, I can see you've got the zone press down perfect, and you're running the break like the old show-time Lakers," Jim said. He was trying to pump them back up after Nate's last outburst. That was pretty obvious.

"We're gonna spend the last few minutes working on our good old basic man-to-man defense," Jim continued. "The second unit plus the coaches against the starting five. Come on, big guys, we're gonna eat you alive."

"In your dreams," Will said with forced enthusiasm. Dave knew that Will was doing his best to act as if nothing had happened. He also noticed that Nate had barely moved since blowing up at Will. He just stood at the corner of the blacktop, arms folded, a sullen look on his face.

Mark was set to trigger the play from out of bounds. Dave stepped in front of him, hands up, trying to make it hard for him to find a target. Out of the corner of his eye, Dave saw Derek sticking to Nate like glue. Then he heard Nate explode again.

"What are you doing playing me man-to-man, Derek, you lamebrain?"

Nobody moved. Nobody breathed.

Derek Roberts, a razor-thin black kid, was without a doubt the best player on the Bulls. He also hardly ever opened his mouth—not to talk trash, not to goof around. Because he was so good, and because he was so quiet, the coaches usually left him alone and let him do his thing.

Brian, who had a short fade haircut and the sweetest fadeaway jumper in the league, finally broke the silence. "Jim told us to play man-to-man, Coach," he said simply. "Just a few seconds ago. That's why Derek was sticking to you."

Dave saw Nate look over at Jim. Jim nodded, as if to say, *Brian's right.*

Nate looked down at his sneakers. "Sorry, man," he mumbled in Derek's direction, without actually looking him in the eye.

Still nobody moved.

"It's pretty hot out here," Jim said, wiping the back of his neck with his palm. "I think maybe we've had enough."

"Yeah, that's it for today," Nate said quickly.

Just "That's it for today"? Dave thought. *No "Let's go get some sodas at my dad's store"? No "You dudes are too good— there's nothin' else I can teach you"?*

Dave knew that something a lot bigger than the Sampton game was bothering Nate. He had no idea what it was, but seeing Nate act like a total stranger gave him a sharp, twisting feeling in the pit of his stomach.

CHAPTER 2

"Yo, Jim," Jo said with a devilish gleam in her eye. "Any idea where that precious basketball is that you always lug around with you?"

"You mean the one he got at that hotshot high-school hoops camp for being voted Mr. Basketball? The one he sleeps with at night?" Will added, winking at his teammates.

"Hey, don't even *think* about telling me you lost that ball," Jim said, looking alarmed. He grabbed for the mesh ball bag Jo was carrying. "C'mon, help me look for it!"

While Jim was frantically emptying

the balls out of the bag, Brian tiptoed up behind him. Brian's belly was bulging, since the "missing" basketball was stuffed under his T-shirt.

"Oh, excuse me!" Brian said as he bumped Jim from behind with the protruding basketball.

Jim whirled around. "I should have known!" he shouted. "You know, you guys . . ." He was trying to yell at them in his coach's "authority" voice, but he couldn't help laughing at the sight of Brian. This often happened to Jim when he was trying to discipline the Bulls. "You guys are a bunch of two-year-olds," he finished with a grin.

"We'll take that as a compliment," Brian said.

Dave was relieved to see that Nate's strange outbursts at practice hadn't brought the Bulls down. They were still as rambunctious as usual as they tromped off the Jefferson Park blacktop court that was their home turf. Since the town of Branford had no community center, the Bulls held all their practices at Jefferson. The downside was that they had to play all their league games on the road. The upside was that the park was right across the street from Bowman's Market, which was owned and operated by Nate Bowman, Sr. The balding, always smiling Mr. Bowman knew more about hoops than just about any other adult they knew.

And Bowman's Market was where they were headed.

"Man, I can't wait to put some moves on those Portsmouth Panthers again," Mark bragged as the Bulls approached the shop. As he walked, Mark was  busy trying to wipe his prescription goggles on his shorts, something he seemed to do at least twenty times an hour.

"I wouldn't get too cocky—we only beat them by five the last time we played them," Will reminded Mark. "And you know what Mr. Bowman would say."

"I know, I know," Mark answered. "Don't count your chickens—"

"Before they're hatched!" the rest of the Bulls chimed in on cue.

"Panthers, shmanthers," Jo said in

her usual no-nonsense way. Though a lot of the Bulls talked a big game, Jo was really the most confident player of all. "We'll take care of the Panthers. Just let me at those Slashers! One more shot at them is all we need."

Dave wasn't surprised by Jo's eagerness for revenge. After all, her wise-guy brother, Otto, who tried to put Jo down every chance he got, was the Slashers' top player. Still, Dave liked what he was hearing. This kind of upbeat trash talk, which always seemed to surface as the Bulls headed to Bowman's, was making him forget how troubled he felt about Nate.

Dave flung the door open. "Yo, Mr. Bowman!" he called. "Set 'em up. Da Bulls are in the house!"

No answer.

"Mr. Bowman?" Dave asked again.
Still no answer.
That was strange. Bowman's Market

was the Bulls' second home. Practice wasn't officially over until they'd downed their share of sodas at Bowman's. In fact, it was Mr. Bowman himself who'd given most of the Bulls their nicknames. Will had become "Too-Tall" as a result of growing four inches after the previous season. Brian was "Fadeaway," partially because of his Scottie Pippen–style haircut, but mostly because of his deadly fadeaway jumper from the baseline. Dave had been dubbed "Droopy" because of his floppy blond hair and his extremely long, baggy shorts.

Dave had never arrived at Bowman's with the Bulls and not found Mr. Bowman waiting for them at the counter. Again, Dave had a sharp, twisting feeling in his stomach. There was no real reason for him to be worried, but ever since his father had died, a few years earlier, he got a little nervous when adults weren't where they were supposed to be.

"Hey, Nate," Will asked, "what's the story here? Did your father take the day off?"

"Yeah, for the first time in history?" Brian joked.

Dave didn't join in the kidding. He

waited anxiously for Nate's answer.

"Dad had to go down to Springfield," Nate finally mumbled. "My cousins just moved there from Decatur. Dad's helping them move in."

Dave thought Nate looked uncomfortable as he spoke.

"Isn't your dad not supposed to do any heavy lifting, with his back problems and being overweight and all?" Dave asked.

"Nah, he just says that to try to make you all feel sorry for him, and to get me to do all the work around the store," Nate answered with a wink, doing his best to sound like his wise-guy self. He started to pass around cans of soda. "You know he's strong as a bull."

"Speaking of which," Brian said, lifting his can of Pepsi, "to the Bulls!"

"To the Bulls!" his teammates toasted, clinking soda cans.

Dave could see that nobody else found Mr. Bowman's absence as troubling as he did. They didn't seem to be the least bit concerned.

But he was getting more and more suspicious. First there were Nate's surprising blowups at practice. Nate was usually pretty easygoing, the kind of guy who could smirk, joke, and low-five on the sidelines when the Bulls were down by ten.

On top of that, Dave didn't find Nate's Springfield story very convincing. He'd known the Bowmans from the time when he used to dribble a basketball with two hands—and he'd never heard about any cousins in Decatur!

When Nate disappeared into the storage room to haul out another case of soda, Dave followed him. "Hey, Nate," he said. "Where's your dad? Really."

"Droopy, man, what is your problem?" Nate asked, still with a forced smile. "He's in Springfield with my aunt and uncle and cousins. You got wax in your ears or something?"

Dave looked Nate straight in the eye. "What aunt and uncle? C'mon, Nate. You expect me to believe that story?"

Nate had been calm ever since the Bulls had left Jefferson, but now he lost it.

"Dave, why don't you just mind your own business for once?" he exploded.

Dave winced at Nate's strong words as Nate stalked out of the storage room.

"What happens to your dad *is* my business," he whispered to Nate, even though his coach had already left.

CHAPTER 3

Dave sat hunched over, elbows on his knees, at the end of the Bulls' bench. Across the gym, the Portsmouth Panthers were getting final instructions from their coach. Dave's own teammates were yapping away, getting themselves psyched, but he barely noticed the commotion.

"Where's Nate?" Dave asked Jim. Hearing the worry in his own voice, he tried to make it sound as if his question was no big deal. "You know I always like to see him jam one before a game. It inspires me to greater heights."

"For you to get to greater heights,"

Will told his shorter teammate, "you don't need Nate, you need a *ladder*." Will hadn't picked up on how concerned Dave was about Nate's absence, and he could never pass up a chance to needle his friend.

"Nate won't be here today," Jim answered. Seeing Dave's face drop, he added, "He's gotta take care of the store. It's just me and you guys against the world."

"No problem, man," Will assured his older brother. "Just get these guys to help me out on the big dude with the buck teeth, and we'll cruise." When the Bulls had beaten Portsmouth 41–36 earlier in the season, the tall center the Bulls called Bucky had been the Panthers' only real offensive threat.

"Yeah," Brian added. "Anyway, Nate doesn't do that much besides intimidating the other team with his backward jams before the game and keeping us loose with those goofy faces he makes. So today we'll just laugh at the Panthers instead."

"You guys may think I do all the coaching and Nate does all the cheerleading," Jim said with a note of seriousness in his voice, "but whether you know it or not, Nate recognizes defenses a lot quicker than I do. I'm gonna miss that big-time."

"Hey, Coach, don't worry about it," MJ said. "I'll take care of that for you today." MJ was as good at reading defenses as anyone—kid or coach.

Dave had barely listened to the last several sentences of the conversation. He was still stuck on *Nate won't be here today. He's gotta take care of the store.* Nate had to help out at the store? That meant Mr. Bowman was still out of town. Either that, or he was somewhere that Nate didn't want to talk about. . . .

Dave shook his head, trying to clear away the troubling thoughts. *I've got to get psyched for this game,* he told himself.

Although the other Bulls were playing their best, Dave just couldn't manage to get with the program. With the score 11–11 and just ten seconds left in the first quarter, Dave lost his man with a crossover dribble but was hammered on his way to the hoop by the Panthers' center. Two shots.

Thirteen-eleven, Dave thought. He had already counted his two free throws as good, because he was usually automatic from the line.

But he was a little soft on the first one, and it bounced off the front rim. Trying to adjust, he put too much on the second shot and bricked it off the back iron.

"Droopy, that's not like you," Jim observed as Dave walked slowly to the bench with his head down. *Next thing he's gonna rag me about is my four turnovers,* Dave thought, but Jim left that unsaid.

"I don't know, Coach," Dave said. "I just can't get into it today."

"Tell you what," Jim said. "Take a rest. Mark, go on in for Dave for a while. We've got to straighten this dude out." He squeezed Dave's shoulder.

In the second quarter, Mark began launching his ugly two-hand heaves from downtown—and hitting them. Derek was on fire, as usual, while Will was scoring easily off Bucky in the paint. Jo and Brian seemed perfectly content dishing the ball off to the three hot hands.

With the Bulls up 30–17, Jim sent Dave back in for Jo to finish out the half. But his first pass, intended for Will, was sloppy, and it wound up in Bucky's hands instead. The big Portsmouth center rambled up the floor, but luckily for Dave, he blew the layup.

Dave wasn't so lucky on the Bulls' final possession. While he was trying to dribble out the clock at the top of the key, he had his pocket picked by the opposing point guard. The quick Panther scurried down the court and converted the layup, closing the gap to 30–19 as the buzzer sounded.

"Dave, what's happening here?" Will wanted to know as the Bulls headed to their bench for halftime. "You trying to save your energy for Sampton or what? C'mon, man, we've got a nice lead, but we still gotta play this game."

Usually Dave would have been ticked off by Will's acting as if he were the coach. But this time Dave didn't even answer him. Instead, he walked up to Jim.

"Coach," he said, "I know you know where Nate really is. Come on, what's the story?"

"Dave," Jim answered firmly, "we'll talk about Nate and his dad later. Right now we've got a second half to get through. You know, you're all talking about next week's Sampton game, but I'm going to tell you something, Droopy. You keep turning the ball over to the Panthers like you did in the first half and there won't *be* any Sampton game!"

We'll talk about Nate and his dad later. Again, that was all Dave had heard. *So there is something wrong with Mr. Bowman,* he concluded. *And we're out here playing a stupid basketball game!*

"Okay, team!" Jim called as the Bulls got ready to take the floor for the second half. "Let's go with the starting five. And I want to see some hustle out there!"

"Hands in!" Brian shouted.

The Bulls formed a circle around their coach, each putting a hand in the middle. At the count of three, they roared, *"Show time!"*

As Dave brought the ball across mid-court on the Bulls' first possession, he saw MJ nudge Jim with his elbow and say something to him. Jim shouted to the Bulls, "The Panthers are in a man-to-man now. Let's see some good picks."

Dave approached the top of the key and passed off to Jo. But then he just stood there.

"Dave!" he heard Jim bellow from the sidelines. "Picks!"

Dave looked over, wondering why Jim sounded so impatient. He hadn't heard Jim call out the first time. Or if he did, it hadn't registered. "Yeah. Picks," Dave repeated.

Jo drove to the hoop for a finger roll, but she put it up too hard, and Bucky grabbed the ball as it rolled off the rim. He threw a beautiful outlet to the point guard, the one who had stripped Dave to end the first half. The guard streaked up for a fast-break layup, and Portsmouth had the first points of the second half.

Dave was staring up into the bleachers when he heard Jo yell, "Yo, Dave! Game's here. I need some help!" She was indicating that she wanted to inbound the ball to him after the Portsmouth basket.

"Sorry," Dave mumbled as he took the pass. He caught sight of Jo looking over at Jim and rolling her eyes.

"C'mon, Dave," Jim called out impatiently. "Snap out of it! Let's play some ball!"

But Dave continued to play as if he were in a trance the entire second half. Fortunately, the rest of the Bulls were clicking, and late in the fourth quarter they held a 56–36 lead.

With three minutes left on the clock, Jo passed the ball in to Dave following a nice jump hook by Bucky.

Dave started dribbling up the floor, his mind wandering. *What if there is something really wrong with Mr. Bowman? Nobody told me what was going on when my dad was sick, either. What would I do if I didn't have Mr. Bowman to cheer me up after a tough game?*

His train of thought was scrambled by the screech of the referee's whistle.

"Ten seconds!" he heard the ref call out. "Panthers' ball!"

Dave felt his face get hot. How embarrassing! A ten-second violation, and nobody had even been pressing him!

"Mark!" Dave heard Jim shout. "Go on in and finish the game for Dave. I don't know *what* he's doing!"

Dave could hardly blame his coach. The ten-second violation call was by no means his only stupid move of the second half. He'd already been whistled three times for traveling. Not to mention that he was two for nine from the line for the game. Normally he hit his free throws at around 85 percent, the best on the Bulls.

Since the Bulls wound up routing the Panthers, 62–38, Dave's zombielike performance didn't receive that much attention on the ride back to Branford.

"Don't you just love it when we crush teams who think they're hot stuff?" Chunky asked from the back of the Bowman's Market van, which was also known as the Bullsmobile.

"Yeah," Brian added. "I heard their macho center saying before the game that we were nothin' and that we were lucky to have beaten 'em the first time. He said Sampton was the only team they had to worry about. Well, guess what, Bucky—now you don't have to worry about Sampton anymore." He waved his hand. "See ya!"

From the driver's seat, Jim just shook his head and laughed.

"I'm telling you guys," Jo said as she tugged her baseball cap into place. "People talk about Sampton like they're the Houston Rockets or something. But we're gonna do to them exactly what we just did to the Panthers. After next Saturday, the Slashers are gonna be *history!*"

Dave, sitting up front next to Jim and staring at his hands, had been only half listening to his teammates. In the midst of all the high-spirited gloating and glorious predictions, he blurted out, "Mr. Bowman's sick, isn't he, Jim?"

All of a sudden the van quieted down. Everybody waited for Jim to answer.

Jim wet his lips. "I've been holding off for the right time to tell you guys," Jim answered, without taking his eyes off the road. "You're right, Dave. Mr. Bowman's had a heart attack. Nate's with him in the hospital right now."

A moment earlier the Bullsmobile had been filled with confident yapping and laughter—the sounds of victory. Now there was total silence.

Dave, in a panic, tried to calm himself by taking a deep breath. But he couldn't do it. He felt as though the wind had been knocked out of him.

"I heard the Bulls' march to the finals continued without me," Nate said with a grin as the team filed into Bowman's. "Think I should feel insulted?" he asked, winking at Jim.

"Nah. You should just be proud you taught them so well," Jim answered. "How'd you get the word so fast?"

"Miracle of the modern telephone," Nate said. "You guys took forever getting back here, so I called the gym at Portsmouth. Man, maybe you can win without old Nate, but it looks like I'm the only one who can book in that Bullsmobile."

31

Nate looked at the Bulls. "All right, guys, don't hold back," he said. "Give me some details."

Brian finally spoke up. "We won, sixty-two to thirty-eight," he said. "We were pretty hot."

"That's great," Nate said, "but remind me not to offer you a job as color commentator when I get to the NBA. I want *details*. What about you, Too-Tall? Did you eat Bucky's lunch?"

"Yeah, I shut him down pretty good," Will said reluctantly.

Nate looked at Will, waiting, but that was all Will said. Then Nate turned his attention to Jim, a questioning look on his face.

"Yeah, I told them, Nate," Jim admitted. "Dave knew something was up."

Nate drew in a deep breath. "Okay," he said, "so now you all know my dad was rushed to the hospital two days ago. That means you forgot how to talk to me?"

"How *is* your dad?" Will asked.

"He's fine. Just fine," Nate answered.

"We're not little kids," Brian said. "You can tell us how he really is."

Nate sighed. "Okay. 'Cautiously optimistic' is how the doctor put it. My dad had a heart attack, but he's in stable condition. We were all really scared yesterday, which was why I was so angry at practice—sorry about that, y'all. But now the doctors think there's a pretty good chance he's going to be all right."

Dave froze when Nate said the words *heart attack*. He couldn't help remembering how crushed he had felt when he'd heard the same words about his father a few years before. And his dad had died in the hospital the very next day. *The same thing could happen to Mr. Bowman,* he thought.

"I'm glad to hear the worst seems to be over, Nate," Jim said.

"All right. Now that you've got the full medical report," Nate continued, "will someone please tell me exactly how you guys destroyed Portsmouth today?"

"Well," Brian said, "Mark was absolutely unconscious from downtown, and Derek was his usual superstar self. And Will actually did do a pretty decent job on Bucky." Then, thumping himself on the chest, he added, "But of course somebody had to get all these hotshots the ball—"

"And that's where I took over," Jo interrupted. "Fifteen assists, at the very least!"

"Glad to see nobody's lost their modesty while I was gone," Nate said, smiling.

How can they keep talking about basketball when Mr. Bowman's in the hospital? Dave wondered.

"The truth is, Nate, they're not exaggerating a whole lot," Jim said. "We got off to a slow start, but then we really got cooking. Derek, Mark, and Will put up the points, and Jo and Brian took care of the dishing. Chunky was a monster on the boards, and MJ bailed me out on the bench, reading the defenses the way you usually do."

"Uh, excuse me, Coach, aren't you forgetting something?" Mark asked Nate, pointing to the soda cans displayed behind the refrigerator's glass door.

Nate hit himself on the forehead with his palm. "Duh! Too much excitement today," he said. "What's my dad's rule? Win by more than twenty, and they're on the house. Okay, cold sodas, coming right up," he said as he headed back to the big refrigerator.

Dave followed him to the back of the store.

"Ol' Droopy Drawers," Nate said, flashing Dave a grin. "Have one of those rare off days today? I didn't hear your name mentioned in the highlights."

"Yeah," Dave answered, "it wasn't my best game."

"No sweat," Nate said, putting a large hand on Dave's shoulder. "You'll light it up next weekend against the Slashers. I'll put money on that."

"That's what I wanted to talk to you about, Nate," Dave said. "I really don't think we should be playing that game next weekend."

Nate stopped pulling cans out of the refrigerator. "What are you talking about, Droopy?"

Dave wet his lips with the tip of his tongue. "I'm saying that until your dad's out of the woods, I don't think we should be playing basketball. I think we ought to be over at the hospital, cheering him up."

Nate thought for a minute, then began carrying the cans out to the front of the store. "Dave," he answered, "my dad's pretty knocked out. He sleeps a lot. He can't really have visitors there for that long. You can go see him, sure—that'd be great. But there's no reason for you guys to stop playing ball."

"Nate, I can't even think about basketball when your dad's in the hospital!" Dave shot back, trailing after his coach. Noticing that the rest of the Bulls were now listening, he lowered his voice. "I think that's a pretty good reason to stop playing."

"Here, give me those," Jo said to Nate, grabbing the cold cans. "If we wait for you guys, we'll all die of thirst." Looking at Dave, she added, "And I heard what you were saying about not playing. I disagree totally. A bunch of guys hanging around Mr. Bowman and looking like the end of the world is coming . . . well, that's about the last thing he needs."

"Is that so?" Dave asked, annoyed that Jo had been listening in on his conversation. "And who made you the expert?"

"All I know," Jo said, "is that when my mom was really sick a few years ago, all she asked about was how I did in gymnastics that day, or how my brother did in basketball. It made her feel better to know that we were doing okay even though she was sick."

Dave rolled his eyes. "*Very* convenient. You'll say anything that gives us an excuse to go ahead and play Sampton."

Jo shot a look at Dave. "You think you're the only one who cares about Mr. Bowman," she said. "Well, I've got a news flash for you. We *all* care about Mr. Bowman. But that doesn't give us an excuse to sleepwalk on the court, like you did today."

Dave tightened his fists but didn't say anything.

"All right, guys," Nate said, holding up his hands. "Let's not get too excited. Besides, this isn't just for you two to fight out. This is a question for *all* the Bulls. So for now let's just drop it, have a few sodas, and celebrate today's win. Then on Monday at practice, we can settle this thing as a team."

Dave and Jo continued to glare at each other.

"All right, Jo?" Nate asked.

"All right," Jo grudgingly agreed.

"All right, Dave?"

Silence.

"I said, *all right*, Dave?" Nate repeated.

Dave clenched his jaw. "Yeah, all right," he said finally.

CHAPTER 5

It's only a basketball game, Dave said to himself as he absently dribbled over to Jefferson Park for practice on Monday. *The league will let us make it up another time. Mr. Bowman needs us. If one of us was sick, you think Mr. Bowman wouldn't be there every minute he could?*

Over and over he rehearsed his arguments. There was no way the rest of the Bulls wouldn't agree with him!

Arriving at the blacktop, he heard Jim already dividing the Bulls into two squads for a scrimmage.

"Mark," Jim said, "since you're a guard and you never saw a shot you didn't like, you get to be Otto Meyerson."

"I wonder if I should take that as a compliment," Mark said as he hoisted up a thirty-footer that just barely hit the rim.

"Somehow I don't think so," Jo replied with a smirk.

"And MJ," Jim continued, "you play forward, and you're built a little like Spider, so why don't you be him?"

"Yeah," Brian joked, "just give him a black wool hat and take away his brain, and he'll be *exactly* like Spider."

Jim looked at Chunky next.

"No!" Chunky said, holding up his hands. "Don't even think about asking me to be Matt, that redheaded nitwit. Anything but that!"

It was the Bulls' first string against their subs and coaches, with the subs playing the part of the Slashers. Jim and Nate often had the Bulls prepare for a big game this way. *Not a bad idea,* Dave thought, *but why now?* Today they had something more important to deal with.

"Hey, Coach," Dave broke in as Jim completed choosing the mock Slashers. "What's going on? I thought we were gonna decide about whether we're playing Saturday's game or not."

"We are," Jim said. "But we're going to practice first and talk later. Once you Bulls get into talking," he added with a laugh, "we can forget about getting anything done."

"But Nate said . . ."

"You're right, Droopy, I did say we'd take care of this thing at practice," Nate agreed. "But Jim and I decided we'd at least get a few drills in before you guys get carried away and break into all-out war."

"Fine," Dave said, annoyed. "But don't think I'm gonna forget about it just because we start playing."

"We'll get to it, Droopy," Nate reassured him. "Don't worry, we'll get to it." Then, to the rest of the team, he said, "Okay, Slashers' ball out!"

MJ inbounded the ball to Mark, who started dribbling upcourt. The moment he passed mid-court, he drew the ball in toward his chest, then heaved it with two hands toward the basket. It fell way short.

"Mark, what was *that?*" Jim shouted.

"You said I was Otto," Mark answered. "Wasn't that typical Otto? If he's open, he shoots. Doesn't matter if he's forty-five feet from the hoop."

Dave saw that Brian was actually rolling on the floor laughing. Will was pretty hysterical, too. *Why do they find this whole thing so amusing?* he wondered.

"Okay, Mark," Nate agreed. "That was a pretty decent Otto imitation. But next time, how about making us work just a little on D before you let fly?"

"You got it, Coach," Mark said, unable to wipe the smile off his face.

Now it was the Bulls' starters' turn on offense. Dave brought the ball up the floor, then passed to Brian. Brian scored easily on a baseline jumper, with the help of a screen set by Derek.

"I can make that shot in my sleep," Brian bragged. "Isn't anybody even gonna put a hand in my face?"

"Hey, we're the Slashers," Chunky reminded him. "You don't expect us to play defense, too, do you?"

After Brian's hoop, Nate dribbled the ball upcourt for the Slashers. As he reached the top of the key, he lowered his head and began barreling toward the hoop.

Will established position in Nate's path, braced himself firmly for the collision—and was sent flying as Nate came hurtling into him.

"Way to take the charge, Will!" Jim shouted, running over to help him up. "Did you see that, guys? That was textbook! Will saw Nate put his head down just the way Spider always does, he got position, and boom! He'll get that charge call every time!"

They continued playing this way for another half hour, the Bulls against the mock Slashers. On defense, the Bulls played a zone. Dave knew that in a real game a zone would force the impatient Slashers to hoist up a lot of long, low-percentage shots. On offense, they worked on setting picks, to take advantage of the Slashers' laziness on defense.

"All right—perfect! That's great!" Jim called out after the Bulls' swarming zone defense forced MJ to put up a twenty-five-footer that thwacked off the backboard. "Let's grab some water. When we come back, we're going to work on our fast break, because you know how slow the Slashers are getting back on D."

While his teammates headed over to the edge of the blacktop for their squeeze bottles, Dave walked up to the two coaches.

"Well?" he said.

"Well what, Droopy?" asked Nate. "What's on your mind?"

"You know what's on my mind," Dave answered. "You said we'd practice first and talk later. Well, now it's later."

Nate and Jim looked at each other. Nate gave a little nod.

As the Bulls drifted back to the blacktop to resume practice, Nate announced, "All right, you guys. You know that Saturday at the store Droopy brought up the idea of not playing any more hoops until my dad is out of the hospital. Did I get that right, Droopy?"

"Exactly," Dave said. "I think being

with Mr. Bowman is more important than a basketball game." Dave looked down at his black hightops, then out at his teammates. "He needs us with him."

"Anybody else feel the way Dave does?" Nate asked.

"Actually, I do," Jim said quietly.

Dave looked at him, surprised. He was lucky to have such an important ally on his side.

"Basically, if we play, Nate, I think it's unfair to you," Jim explained. "If you come to the game, you'll spend the whole time worrying about your dad. If you don't come, you'll miss the most important game of the season. It's not right."

There was silence for a few seconds. Then another voice, soft but forceful, said, "I'm with Dave and Jim. Mr. Bowman comes first. Basketball is second."

It was Derek! Dave couldn't believe his ears. Derek hardly ever opened his mouth, but when he did, what he said carried a lot of weight.

"Okay, what about the other side?" Nate said. "Dime, I know you're in favor of playing. Want to tell us why?"

Jo answered without hesitation. "It's

like I said the other day about my mom. When she was sick, it made her feel good to know life was going on. My gut feeling says Mr. Bowman would feel exactly the same way."

"I've got to agree with you," Nate said quietly. Then with a smile he added, "And I think I know the guy pretty well."

"Well, I'd say that ought to settle it," Will said. "If his own son thinks we should play, then we should play."

Dave felt his face getting hot. He hated when Will acted like such a know-it-all. "Will, let's face it. All you want to do is play the Slashers on Saturday!"

Will stared at Dave. "You know, Dave," he said, "everyone's pretty sick of your—"

"All right, enough!" Nate cut in, no longer smiling. "You've all had a chance to talk. Now let's put it to a vote. All those in favor of not playing any more basketball until my dad's out of the hospital?"

Dave put his hand up high and saw Jim and Derek raise theirs, too. A split second later Brian's hand also went up. Dave gave Brian a grateful look. He glanced around at the rest of the team, but those four hands were the only ones that went up.

"All those in favor of going ahead and playing on Saturday?" Nate asked, raising his own hand. Jo and Will followed quickly. Then Dave saw Mark raise his hand. Then Chunky. Then MJ.

"Thanks a lot, guys," Dave said sarcastically to the last few Bulls. "You really stood up for what you believe in."

"Dave, cut it out!" Nate scolded. "Maybe they did vote for what they believe in. Not everyone has to think the same way you do."

"Okay, it's a done deal," Jim concluded. "We'll practice the rest of this week, and we'll play Sampton on Saturday, as scheduled."

"Yeah," Dave said as he started backing away from the blacktop. "Mr. Bowman could be dying, but we're not going to let that get in the way of our fun."

"Hey, Droopy," Nate objected, "nobody said my dad's dying. Besides, where do you think you're off to? We've still got a practice going on here."

"I don't know . . . all of a sudden I feel kind of sick to my stomach just being around you guys," Dave replied over his shoulder as he walked away.

CHAPTER 6

Dave hurried anxiously to the end of the clean, white hospital hallway. The smell of disinfectant was overpowering. He saw a man coming in the opposite direction wearing a green scrub suit and those paper shoes everyone in hospitals seemed to have.

"Which way to cardiology, please?" Dave asked, hoping he didn't sound quite as desperate as he felt.

Without stopping, the doctor said, "First hallway, turn left. Then through the double doors."

Dave made the left, then looked up over the doors. CARDIOLOGY, the plate read.

He saw room 302 first, then 304, then 306—the room he was looking for. He peeked in.

Although a curtain was drawn half-way around the bed, Dave could see Mr. Bowman. He looked a lot smaller and skinnier than Dave remembered him. His eyes were closed, and he didn't seem to be moving at all. *Is he breathing?* Dave wondered, beads of sweat breaking out on his own forehead.

Then Mr. Bowman's eyes opened.

"Droopy," he said with a small smile. Dave thought his voice sounded strange. "I'm so glad you stopped by. You know, I was just thinking about the last time I saw the Bulls play—and now I open my eyes, and there you are! How's it going, Droopy? Nate tells me you boys blew those Portsmouth Panthers right out of their own gym!"

Dave was glad to hear Mr. Bowman's energy level pick up as he talked about the Bulls. Now he sounded like the real Mr. Bowman.

"Nate got that right—it was show time!" Dave answered, trying to appear upbeat even though being in a hospital room felt weird and scary. "You know the Panthers can't touch us when we're playing our game."

"And how about you, Droopy?" Mr. Bowman asked. "Did you have your typical Grant Hill all-star performance that we've come to expect?"

"Sure did," Dave lied. "Probably thirty-five points. At least a dozen assists. Maybe ten boards. Triple-double. You know, the usual." *Mr. Bowman doesn't really need to know I got called for just about every violation in the book and that I spent half the game on the bench,* Dave thought.

"Well, that's great," Mr. Bowman said with a smile, "because I know you've got the Slashers coming up on Saturday, and you want to have some momentum going for you. Practice going good?"

"Perfecto," Dave answered. "We're cranking up our fast break, fine-tuning the zone press . . ." Dave's voice trailed off in the middle of the sentence. *Enough of this phony enthusiasm!* he thought.

"Mr. Bowman," Dave went on, his voice dropping to a lower level. His throat felt very dry. "Why are we just talking about basketball, like it's the only thing going on?"

"What do you mean, Droopy?" Mr. Bowman asked.

"I mean . . ." He felt the tears wanting to come out, and he clenched his jaw to hold them back. "I mean . . . who *cares* about the Bulls? We miss seeing you at the store after practice, Mr. Bowman. We miss hearing you cheer at the games."

Finally the tears started coming. Dave couldn't help it. "I'm worried about you, Mr. Bowman!" he sobbed.

Dave was sitting on the edge of the bed, and Mr. Bowman put a hand on his shoulder. "Dave, Dave," Mr. Bowman consoled, "Branford Hospital is one of the best in the state. And Dr. Gartner is the top cardiologist around. I couldn't be in better hands. There's nothing to worry about."

"Why does everyone pretend there's nothing to worry about?" Dave choked. He wasn't concerned about crying anymore, and the tears flowed freely. "There *is* something to worry about."

"Here, Dave, have a tissue," Mr. Bowman said, reaching for the box on his bedside table.

"Mr. Bowman," Dave said, "my dad died of a heart attack. You know that, right?"

"Sure, Dave, I know. Everyone in town felt terrible."

"Yeah," Dave said, "but not as terrible as I felt."

"Of course not," Mr. Bowman agreed.

"No, that's not what I mean," Dave said. "The night my dad died? That afternoon we had an argument over my allowance. He wouldn't give me a raise I thought I deserved, so I called him a cheapskate."

"Dave," Mr. Bowman said softly, "kids say stuff like that to their parents all the time. Parents are used to that. I'll tell you, Nate's called me a lot worse than cheapskate!"

"But it wasn't only that," Dave went on. "I'd been acting like a jerk the whole week. You know, I thought it was cool to be mean to my dad. But I always thought I'd have the chance to make it up to him. Man, *now* I sure wish I had some more time to spend with him."

"So *that's* it," Mr. Bowman said, nodding his head. "You're afraid I'm going to die, and you want to make sure you spend a lot of time with me first?"

"I didn't say that. . . ." Somehow, hearing Mr. Bowman say it, it didn't sound quite right.

"Dave," Mr. Bowman said warmly, "I'm really glad you feel that way, but I'm not planning on leaving you guys so soon. Sure, the doctors think I'm still a little bit touch-and-go, but I'm confident I'll be out of this joint by early next week."

"Fine," Dave said. "Then the Bulls'll visit you every day until you're home."

"You guys can visit me every day," Mr. Bowman replied. "My pleasure. But visiting hours are limited, you know. There's no reason you can't keep playing basketball. If you missed the Slashers game on my account, I'd shoot myself." Seeing Dave flinch, Mr. Bowman laughed and said, "Excuse the expression."

"I'm sorry," Dave said, "but I'm not going to play a basketball game while you're still in the hospital."

A tall nurse with a no-nonsense expression ducked her head into the room. "Sorry, visiting hours are over," she said, looking at Dave. "Time to let the patient get some rest."

Mr. Bowman took Dave's hand and smiled at him. "Droopy, you know I'm closer to you than I am to any of the other Bulls. You know I think of you like a son."

Dave felt the pressure on his hand. "I know that, Mr. Bowman."

"Then do me a favor," Mr. Bowman said, "for my sake. Play the game."

Dave swallowed hard and forced a smile. "I'll do my best, Mr. Bowman," he said. But he knew it wasn't going to be easy.

CHAPTER 7

Even before the pregame warm-ups began, Dave could feel a sense of anticipation in the huge, spanking new Sampton Community Center. For one thing, there were about three times as many people in the bleachers as usual, and the noise level was really turned up—like at a rock concert.

He also counted at least half a dozen black-and-gold Slashers banners, and about an equal number in black and red for the Bulls. *Well*, Dave thought, *this is, after all, the biggest rivalry in the league. And this game is the championship finals.* As Mr. Bowman would say, they were playing for all the marbles.

Dave seemed to be the only person in the gym who wasn't really into it.

The crowd was so loud that Dave could barely hear Jim call out, "Two lines for layups!" Derek led the Bulls onto the court, swooping gracefully to the hoop and laying the ball in gently off the glass. Will followed with another textbook layup, nothing fancy, no wasted motion.

As Dave got ready for his turn, he heard a familiar, obnoxious voice from the Sampton end of the court. "Well, look who's here, the little gymless wonders from Branford. Hey, guys, this place may not be as cozy as your little dump over at Jefferson, but we call it home."

Sure enough, there was Otto Meyerson, greasy crew cut and all, jeering at the Bulls—as usual. Dave looked at Brian and rolled his eyes.

"Ignore the creep," Brian said, shaking his head. "He can't help it. Must be in his genes."

"Hey," Jo said, "leave the rest of the family out of it. Otto managed to become a jerk all on his own."

Dave charged to the hoop, trying to soar extra high, but he put the ball up too hard against the backboard, and it bounced off the rim. He was the first Bull to miss a layup. Chunky rebounded the ball and tossed it to Jo.

She dribbled once behind her back before laying it neatly in.

"Very smooth, Otto Junior," Spider called out sarcastically from the Slashers' end. Dave couldn't believe that even in this sweltering gym Spider was wearing his black wool cap.

"Yo, Hopwood," Spider continued, calling out to Will, "I've noticed you guys are big on drafting little sisters. I have one, too, you know. She's only three, and she's still in diapers, but the Bulls could probably use her. Want me to ask?"

Matt, a short kid with a mop of red hair, slapped Spider five.

"Those two deserve each other, don't they?" Will said to Brian.

"Yeah, kind of like Beavis and Butthead," Brian agreed.

Dave noticed Mr. White, the Slashers' coach, trying to make a big show of disciplining his team. "Spider, Matt, come on now," he said. "We're the host team. I want you men to act like good sports."

"Yeah, right!" Will laughed to his teammates. "He's the one who got his brother to ref the championship game last year, and he's talking about being a good sport!"

Jim had the Bulls move into a semi-circle around the perimeter for a shoot-around. He stayed under the hoop to grab the rebounds and funnel them back out to the shooters.

Dave was still thinking about how annoying Mr. White was when a ball thudded off his chest.

"Come on, Dave," Jim said, "let's stop dreaming."

Just then one of the referees, a short African American man with an athletic build, called both coaches over. After the conference Jim hustled back to the Bulls, telling them the game would be starting in a couple of minutes. As they huddled they heard Matt calling out some garbage about the Slashers owning the Bulls.

"Can somebody just tape his mouth shut?" Will wondered aloud.

"Let him yap all he wants," Brian said. "We'll see who's woofin' when the game is over."

"Okay, guys," Jim warned, "let's not get sucked into that trash talk stuff. We're just going to play our game. Did you see that ref I was talking to? His name is Ron Sparks, and he's the best there is. Mr. Spinelli, the tall one with the mustache, is good, too. So we don't have to worry about any monkey business, like last year."

"You mean the Slashers are going to try to beat us fair and square?" said Jo. "That doesn't sound like them."

"Hey, we haven't played the game yet," Brian cautioned. "You never know what those lamebrains are going to pull."

"All right," Jim said, trying to focus their attention. "We're going to start off in a zone, as you know. And MJ's going to help me again, since Nate'll be a little late."

Dave felt a chill shoot through him. "Excuse me?" he asked. "Nate told us he'd definitely be here today!"

60

"And he will, Dave," Jim assured him. "Hold on to your shorts."

For my sake, play the game, Mr. Bowman had told him. All day long Dave had been trying to get a grip on himself. Now he felt that grip slipping away.

"Did something else happen to Mr. Bowman?" Dave demanded.

"No," Jim said sternly, starting to lose patience. "I said Nate will be here. And by the way, he asked me to give you a message. 'Focus on the game, Dave.' That's what he told me to tell you."

Dave just stared at Jim. Jim stared back. Finally Dave looked down.

"One last thing," Jim added, talking to the whole team again. "I don't think I have to tell you what this game means. This is the *championship,* and these are the *Slashers*. They beat us last year in the finals. They beat us a few weeks ago during the regular season—"

"We beat 'em in that grudge match at the beginning of the summer," Brian offered.

"That doesn't mean squat," Jim snapped, annoyed at Brian for interrupting. "This is payback time. This time we shut the Slashers down for the *season*. And remember," he continued, now looking at Dave, "*focus*. You're gonna give it your all and prove you're the best. Because if you don't, and you lose, sitting around tomorrow wishing you'd tried harder isn't gonna change anything."

Jim put his right hand into the middle of the circle. The rest of the Bulls did the same. "Okay," Jim said, "loud enough so they can hear us back in Branford. One, two, three . . ."

"*Show time!*" they shouted.

"Go get 'em!" Jim yelled.

Dave shuffled out to the painted circle at mid-court. "Let's go, Slashers!" someone yelled, and Dave looked up to see the bleachers filled with black and gold. For reassurance, he looked across to the Bulls' side. The stands there were packed, too. It didn't look as though another person could squeeze into the gym. He could make out his mother sitting next to Brian's parents and little brother and sister. And all around them were the families and friends of the other Bulls, including Derek's father, a famous former player in the NBA. Just seeing them up there made him feel a little better.

"Yo, Danzig, guess who's guarding you today." Otto sidled up to him at the circle. "Just remember," Otto said in a menacing whisper, "I know all your moves." He poked Dave in the ribs. "*All* of 'em."

As the referee Jim had identified as Mr. Sparks got ready to toss the ball, Dave heard Otto say, "Hey, what's up? Only one coach today? No dynamic duo? I thought Branford's high-school All-Americans went everywhere together. Nate finally get sick of you losers?"

Dave felt his face turn red. "You know something, Otto? You're really low," he hissed. He felt ready to explode, but he knew that was exactly what Otto wanted him to do. He tried something like this every game.

Mr. Sparks sent the ball into the air, and Will outleapt Ratso, the Slashers' gawky new center. Dave grabbed the tip and lofted the ball up to Derek, who was gliding toward the basket.

But Spider, who'd seen the play coming, picked off the pass and fired it back to Ratso, who hadn't moved from midcourt. Ratso ambled toward the Slashers' hoop and laid the ball in before the Bulls could get back on defense.

"Slashers! Slashers!" The Sampton bleachers were erupting in noise.

All right, Dave thought as he dribbled upcourt. *So they scored the first basket. It's not like they've won the game already!*

"Yo, Danzig." It was Otto, who was pressing him full-court. *Fine, let him,* Dave thought. Otto couldn't steal the ball from him if his life depended on it, and he'd wear himself out trying.

"One little hoop, Danzig, and your coach already wants time out."

Dave stole a glance over at Jim, but that was all the time Otto needed. He flicked the ball away from Dave and streaked up to the Slashers' basket for an easy layup.

Dave was sure every set of eyes in the gym was staring at him. How could he have fallen for such a dumb trick?

"Slashers! Slashers!" The crowd was even louder than before.

It only got worse. Brian missed an eight-foot baseline jumper that was normally money in the bank. Jo blew an easy open shot from the right of the foul line. The Bulls seemed to be coming apart at the seams.

Dave tried to settle his team down with a sure thing—some free throws. He drove hard to the hoop and managed to draw contact from Otto. Two shots.

But his two-for-nine performance in the Panthers game was still on his mind, and his first shot fell way short—an air ball. As the Slashers hooted, Dave lined up his second shot. Short again, though this time at least he hit the rim.

Before Jim desperately shouted for time, the Bulls had fallen behind 12–0.

"What the heck are you guys doing out there?" Dave could see the veins popping in Jim's neck. "*This* is

the game we've been waiting for? It doesn't look like it! Do I have to remind you that this is the *championship?* How am I going to explain this to Nate when he gets here?"

Jim managed to calm himself down. He slowly reviewed the give-and-go, setting picks, working the ball into the pivot—the fundamentals that had always worked well for the Bulls.

"Okay," he said finally, "we're gonna start chipping away, a little at a time. You're not going to go out and get twelve points back on the first play. Be patient."

Without even meaning to, Dave looked toward the entrance of the gym.

Jim noticed Dave's glance. "Dave . . . ," he warned.

Dave nodded back. *Focus.*

The Bulls had possession. It took four passes, but they were able to work the ball into Will for a short turnaround jumper that was good. Now it was 12–2.

At the other end, the Bulls tightened up their zone defense. Matt finally forced up a heave that was way off. Derek grabbed the rebound.

The Bulls, again, were patient. They

passed the ball around deliberately. Will set a screen, and Brian got off a smooth jumper. 12–4.

By the end of the quarter the score was 15–8, Slashers. The Bulls, as Jim had suggested, were creeping back a little bit at a time. Dave noticed that the Bulls' momentum had taken the steam out of the Sampton crowd.

At the start of the second quarter, Derek isolated Spider in the corner, froze him with a couple of ball fakes, then blew by him for the layup. Now the Bulls fans were on their feet, roaring.

Matt quieted the crowd a little by hitting a short jumper over Jo. Jo quickly inbounded the ball to Dave, who began bringing it up the floor. He eyed the clock.

Six minutes until halftime, and still no Nate. *Hey, maybe it's not an emergency*, Dave thought. *Maybe Nate just had to take care of the store again. Mr. Bowman didn't really look all that bad yesterday—*

SCREECH!

A piercing whistle brought Dave back to the game. Mr. Spinelli, the ref with the mustache, called, "We've got a travel here," and grabbed the ball from Dave. "Gold ball on the side!"

"Come on, Dave, get in the game!" he heard Jim bellow. He knew he deserved it. What had he contributed so far? A couple of turnovers, a bunch of blown foul shots, and a so-so defensive job on Otto.

He wasn't surprised to find himself on the bench a minute later, alongside Chunky and MJ. Jim had sent Mark in for him.

Following the Bulls' burst, the Slashers went on a hot streak of their own, erasing the gains the Bulls had made. Then the game settled into a pattern of trading baskets. Neither the Bulls nor the Slashers could seem to get any real momentum going.

The half ended with the Slashers ahead 26–19, the same seven-point lead they'd had after the first quarter. The fans on the visitors' side seemed to be getting impatient. Except for that one short run late in the first quarter and one early in the second, the Bulls didn't look like a team playing for the champion-ship. Without Dave playing at his best and keeping the team's energy level high, the Bulls were no match for the Slashers.

As they trudged off to the locker room, Jim put his arm around Dave's shoul-ders. "Come on, Dave," he said, "let's see some spirit! We're only down seven. That's nothing! You hit a couple from the line, we're right back in this thing."

Dave didn't answer.

Shaking his head, Jim moved on to try to rally the other Bulls. Dave, alone now, took the opportunity to steal one last desperate glance at the gym's main entrance.

But there was no sign of Nate.

CHAPTER 8

Jo, Brian, Derek, and Chunky sat slumped on a bench between two rows of lockers. Mark and MJ were sprawled on the cold concrete floor, their backs against the wall, as if they were watching TV—though all they were doing was staring straight ahead.

"Ah, this kills," Will grumbled as he stood by the sink with an ice pack on his hand. He'd jammed his right middle finger just before the half ended.

Dave wandered from the bench to the door to the lockers, not quite knowing what to do with himself. *It's weird,* Dave thought. Normally Will or Jo would pipe up, get things going. But nobody seemed to have anything to say. *I'm probably bringing them all down. This is where Nate would come in handy; he'd find a way to loosen things up!*

"Where's Jim?" Brian asked, breaking the silence.

"Telephone," Will answered absently, still concentrating on his injury.

Jo got up off the bench, grabbed a basketball, and out of habit started spinning it on her right index finger. "We keep playing like this," she said, "and it's gonna be a long winter for me." The  ball spun off her finger and thudded to the floor. "Can you imagine living in the same house with Otto if the Slashers kick our butts again? I don't even want to think about it."

"It's simple," MJ blurted out. "All we gotta do is rebound better. The Slashers are missing tons of shots. We've just got to grab those 'bounds."

"Oh, that's all there is to it?" Will

replied sarcastically as he tried to flex his jammed finger. "I'll try to remember that."

"We ought to try to get the ball to Derek and Will down low," Mark volunteered. "At least they're hitting."

"Yeah, maybe," Will answered, "but you guards have to start making a few from the outside. Otherwise the whole defense'll be packed in under the hoop." He tossed the disposable ice pack into a big green plastic garbage can. "Hey," he added, giving Dave a playful swat on the back, "maybe Danzig will surprise everyone and hit a shot or two before the game's over."

Dave gave Will a nasty look. "Don't blame me. While you guys were out there looking sorry in the second quarter, I wasn't even in the game."

Jo couldn't resist. "Hate to say it, Dave, but you weren't in the game even when you were *in* the game."

Everyone laughed.

Dave wasn't smiling. "I told you all we shouldn't have played today," he said in a huffy tone.

"Yeah, you did tell us that," Will replied. "At least a hundred times."

Jim reappeared in the locker room. He'd heard the last few remarks.

"Dave," Jim said in a level, no-nonsense voice, "I've said this before and I'll say it again. You've got to stop moping, put all that stuff aside, and *play*."

Dave refused to look at Jim. He just stared up at the ceiling.

"We've got sixteen minutes of basketball left," Jim continued, speaking to the whole team, "and if we don't pick it up, we're gonna have to sit around and watch the Slashers scoop up that championship trophy for the second year in a row. I guarantee that won't be a pretty sight."

"Coach," MJ suggested, "maybe we ought to shake things up a little. You know, show them a different look."

"You're right, MJ," Jim agreed. "Let's go out and press them full-court, right from the start. Maybe force a few quick turnovers."

"Absolutely," Brian agreed. "We gotta show them we're ready to *take* that trophy!"

"Let's also fast-break every chance

we get," Jim continued. "Catch them napping. I know it's tiring, but we've got three fresh bodies on the bench."

The team continued to look at Jim expectantly.

"Hey, guys," Jim said, "what else do you want? I'm a coach, not a cheerleader. You know I can't make those stirring locker room speeches."

Just then the door to the locker room burst open.

Dave's heart skipped a beat. It was Nate!

Nate was grinning from ear to ear. "Have no fear, Bulls fans," he boomed in a hearty voice brimming with confidence. "I've got someone with me who *can* make those speeches!"

Then Nate made a dramatic, sweeping gesture with his arm, like an emcee introducing the guest of honor. And sure enough, following Nate through the door was Mr. Bowman himself!

"Sorry, no autographs today," Mr. Bowman said, beaming, as he was swarmed by the eager Bulls.

Dave hung back for a moment, his eyes filling with tears. It was too good to be true.

"And no speeches today, either," Mr. Bowman continued, laughing. "Hey, I just got out of the hospital this morning, and I'm a little out of breath."

Dave immediately scooped up a stool and brought it over, but Mr. Bowman waved it away with a smile.

"Now listen," he said to the whole team, in a surprisingly husky voice, "all I want to say is, if I could get myself out of that hospital bed and escape all those doctors and nurses so I could see this game, the least you can do for me is give Sampton a good old-fashioned butt-kicking!"

"You got it!" Will promised.

"Just sit back and watch while we take them apart!" Jo added.

Dave couldn't take his eyes off the man standing in the middle of all this commotion, laughing and joking. Maybe he looked a few pounds lighter, but it was the same old Mr. Bowman.

"All right, guys," Nate bellowed, "talk is cheap. It's time for the Bulls to show those Sampton sissies what's up! And Nate the Great is gonna go out there with you and jam a few—you know, to kind of set the tone."

"Wait, one more thing before you go," Mr. Bowman called to the team. "Just don't make the finish too exciting. You don't want to give me another heart attack!"

"Don't you worry, Mr. Bowman," Brian promised. "We'll blow them out early, just for you."

"Come on, let's go!" Nate yelled. "Hands in, Bulls!"

Dave had never felt more ready to play a game in his life. He was the first to stick out his hand. One by one, each member of the team put a 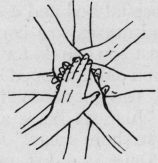 hand on top of Dave's in the center of the circle. "One . . . two . . . three . . . ," they chanted. *"Show time!"*

The Bulls charged out onto the floor behind Nate. Dave and Jim followed more slowly, walking with Mr. Bowman.

"Mr. Bowman," Dave said hesitantly, "remember in the hospital when you asked me to do you a favor and play the game? Well, I tried—I really did. But I just couldn't buy a hoop in the first half."

Mr. Bowman scratched his bald head, thinking for a minute. "Let me give you a suggestion," he said. Turning to Jim, he added, "If Coach doesn't mind."

Jim nodded.

"Here's what I'm thinking," Mr. Bowman said. "Poor Droopy had a lot on his mind in the first half, with his old buddy in the hospital and all. How about in the second half, just for a change, we let Jo handle the point and leave Dave free to concentrate on his shooting?"

"Sounds good to me," Jim agreed.

Dave eagerly nodded, a confident smile on his face.

"You never know," said Mr. Bowman, winking at Dave. "That golden touch may just come back with old Mr. B. up in the bleachers."

CHAPTER 9

No way it was this noisy in the first half, Dave thought.

The cheering from both sides of the gym as the two teams took the floor in the second half had become deafening. It almost seemed as if the fans wanted to get *into* the game rather than just watch it.

Otto sauntered over to Dave, nodding casually in the direction of the Bulls' bench. "I see you've got big, bad Nate Bowman back," he said. "That supposed to impress me?"

"Meyerson," Dave answered, "why would any of us care about what impresses you? And by the way," he added, "your fly's open."

Otto quickly looked down, then realized he was wearing gym shorts.

Dave just snickered and shook his head.

"Bulls' ball," Ron Sparks called out, holding the basketball out to Dave. He blew the whistle to start the second half. Dave inbounded the ball to Jo.

"Whoa, Danzig," Otto said with a smirk as he jogged backward up the court, facing Dave. "What have we here? They don't trust you to bring the ball up anymore? Now *that's* a dis!" Counting on his fingers, Otto continued, "Let's see. You can't shoot, you can't dribble—what exactly *can* you do, Danzig?"

Dave wasn't even tempted to answer. He'd *show* Otto just what he could do!

Jo crossed mid-court and rifled a two-hand chest pass into Will, who was guarded by Ratso. Otto slid over to double-team Will. That left Dave free at the top of the key.

As soon as Will sensed the double-team, he kicked the ball out to Dave. Dave took his time, squared up, and fired. The shot felt perfect as it left his hand.

TWO POINTS!

Dave winked at Otto. "Nice D," he said. Otto had no response.

"Way to hit it!" a husky voice called out from the Branford bleachers. Dave didn't even need to look. He knew it was Mr. Bowman.

Matt stepped behind the baseline to toss the ball in to Otto. But Dave, knowing the Slashers were often sloppy with their inbounds passes, stepped in front of Otto and grabbed the ball. Since he made the steal right under the Bulls' basket, he was able to put in the layup without even having to dribble.

Otto and Matt stood there pointing at each other until Mr. Spinelli finally handed Matt the ball, blew the whistle, and said, "Play!"

The two quick Bulls' hoops had shrunk the Slashers' lead to three, and it was now 26–23. The Slashers began to play with a little more purpose. Working the ball around the perimeter with unusual patience, they were able to get Spider free for a ten-foot base-line jumper. He canned it to make it 28–23.

But the Bulls came roaring right back. Jo dribbled the ball quickly into the frontcourt and then, as Matt put pressure on her, hit Dave with a bounce pass. Dave sent a two-hand, over-the-head bullet to Will at the foul line, then took off for the hoop, leaving Otto glued to the floor.

Dave caught the return pass from Will in full stride and went up for what looked like an easy layup. But Ratso, seeing Dave unguarded, slid over and swatted Dave on his shooting arm.

Mr. Sparks came flying into the lane like a striped bird, his right arm up, his left arm pointing at Ratso. "Number forty-two, gold," he announced, indicating the foul on the Slashers' center. "Two shots."

Dave stepped calmly to the line. With two hands, he gave the ball a slight underhand toss, but with just enough reverse spin so that it bounced right back to him. He flexed his knees twice, positioned the ball with the fingertips of his right hand on the seam, then eyed the front of the rim. He released the ball with plenty of arc and perfect rotation.

Mr. Sparks retrieved the ball and handed it to Dave for his second shot.

Same ritual. Same release. Same result.

"The golden touch!" Dave heard Mr. Bowman cheer.

It had seemed to Dave there'd been a lid on the basket throughout the first half. Now the rim looked as big and inviting as a Hula-Hoop.

The Slashers' lead was back down to three, 28–25. Dave had scored the Bulls' first six points of the third quarter.

Less than ten seconds after Brian slapped Dave a low five, however, Matt froze Jo with a sweet shake-and-bake move and coasted in for an easy layup. The hoop bumped the Slashers' lead back up to five points.

As off-target as both teams had been in the second quarter, that's how hot they were in the third. The scoring came fast and furious. But the result was the same: Neither team could pull away.

With twenty seconds remaining in the period, the Slashers held on to a 42–37 lead. Jo and Dave passed the ball back and forth at the top of the key, holding for the last shot. Otto and Matt seemed content to give them the long one. As a matter of fact, the Slashers' guards almost seemed to be daring Jo or Dave to let fly.

Just as the buzzer was about to sound, Dave checked his feet to make sure he was standing outside the three-point arc. Then he sent up a one-hander, with lots of rotation and perfect follow-through. He knew it was good as soon as it left his fingertips.

THREE FROM DOWNTOWN!

The Bulls fans rose to their feet, stomping on the bleachers.

"The boy can't miss!" Chunky screamed from the sidelines. MJ and Mark were standing on either side of Chunky, cheering wildly.

At the end of the third quarter, the score was Slashers 42, Bulls 40. The Bulls had scored an amazing twenty-one points in the third quarter. Dave had eleven of those points himself.

"Why couldn't you guys shoot like that before?" Jim asked, grinning, as the team huddled around the Bulls' bench between quarters.

"Hey," Nate said, winking at the team, "guess you just needed some cool dude around who can relate to these younger players. You know, bring out the best in them."

"Yeah, I'm sure that must be it," Jim said with a laugh.

The shooting exhibition continued in the fourth quarter. Matt and Spider were on fire for the Slashers. Brian, Jo, and Dave were hitting from all angles for the Bulls.

With three minutes to go in the game, Jo brought the ball up for the Bulls, who were behind 51–50. Reaching the top of the key, she drilled a hard bounce pass to Dave. Dave faked left, then drove right, moving behind a pick set by Derek. Otto saw the pick and slid through it, staying with Dave all the way. As Dave went up for the jumper, Otto got a piece of it. But he also got a piece of Dave's hand.

Mr. Spinelli blew the whistle, raising his hand and pointing at Otto.

Dave settled himself at the foul line. Though all the Bulls fans were stomping and shouting, one voice was clear above the rest. "Droopy," he heard Mr. Bowman call out, *"concentrate."*

Dave spun the ball away from him and let it bounce back, as he always did. He blotted out the cheering. He blotted out the score. He flexed his knees once, then twice. Otto made some wisecrack, but Dave didn't hear it. He fixed his eyes on the front of the rim and released the ball.

His second shot was perfect, too. The Bulls had their first lead of the game, 52–51.

They never gave up another point.

The last three minutes could have been a Bulls' highlights film. On defense, Derek had two monster blocks and Will had one. Jo and Dave each made a steal. Offensively, Dave drilled two more long-range shots, and Derek and Brian each nailed a jumper.

Beginning with Dave's two free throws, the Bulls reeled off the last ten points of the game. The final score was 60–51.

When the buzzer sounded, the Bulls raced over and swarmed their coaches. Then, arms around each other, the entire team swirled around the floor. Bulls fans poured out of the bleachers to join the celebration. Dave couldn't help grinning widely as he was mobbed by his teammates and the crowd.

The dancing and cheering were interrupted by the sound of a man clearing his throat over the PA system. It was the league president, getting ready to present the second-place trophy.

Jim and Nate had a hard time settling the team down, but they insisted that the Bulls clap politely as an expressionless Otto Meyerson shuffled up to accept the runner-up trophy for the Slashers.

But the Bulls went crazy again when the league official reached for the huge first-place trophy. He needed two hands to hold it up in front of his chest.

"And now," the president announced, "the new champions of the Danville County Basketball League, *the Branford Bulls!*"

As the Bulls received a standing ovation, Nate pointed to Dave. "Droopy, you had a pretty decent second half. Why don't you see if you can go up and carry that big piece of hardware back to us without dropping it?"

Dave felt goose bumps on his skin as he accepted the trophy for the Bulls. The Branford fans continued to roar. Dave gathered Will and Brian and the rest of the Bulls around him and whispered something to them. Then he held up his hand to try to quiet the crowd.

As he got ready to speak, he felt his heart pounding. He realized it was easier to make a few remarks to his teammates than to give a speech to a whole crowd. The trophy he held with two hands over his head felt as if it weighed a ton.

"On behalf of the Bulls," Dave said, his voice shaking just a little, "I'd like to present this trophy to our MVP—Mr. Nate Bowman, Senior!"

The Bulls fans continued to roar and applaud, even louder than before.

Mr. Bowman, his face very serious, stepped forward to accept the trophy. He cleared his throat several times, as if he were about to start speaking, but nothing came out. Nate went over and put his long arm around his father's shoulder.

"I just want to say . . . ," Mr. Bowman started. "I just want to say . . ." Dave saw Mr. Bowman swallow hard a few times. He was pretty sure he also saw a tear in the corner of his eye. Mr. Bowman put his fingers to his cheek.

"Thanks," Mr. Bowman finally blurted.

* * *

As the two teams were packing up their gym bags, Dave saw Otto heading in their direction. He was sure Otto had one of his half-witted wisecracks to offer.

"Yo, sis, want a ride home with Mom and Dad?" Otto asked Jo.

Jo looked at her brother suspiciously. Usually if Otto said anything at all to her in public, it was something obnoxious.

"No, thanks," she answered, still wary. "I'm going over to Bowman's Market to celebrate with the Bulls. Tell Mom and Dad I'll be home later."

Otto shuffled his feet and looked down. "You played all right today," he said to his sister.

A smile slowly spread across Jo's face. She couldn't help it.

"And you, Danzig," Otto continued. "What got into you in the second half?"

Dave looked over at Mr. Bowman and smiled. "Oh, some guy just gave me a little suggestion at halftime," he answered. "No big deal."

There was silence. All the Bulls were looking at Otto. He shrugged and, without saying another word, ambled off to where Spider and Matt were waiting for him.

"That wasn't really Otto Meyerson, was it?" Will asked in amazement when Otto was out of earshot.

Jo laughed. "Every once in a while he forgets he's supposed to act like a jerk," she explained. "Don't worry. It'll pass."

"I hope so," Brian said, shaking his head. "I like him better when he's a pain in the butt."

"Yeah," Chunky agreed, "it's cooler to beat the Slashers when we can hate them. What's he trying to do, ruin all our fun?"

The team headed out to the parking lot, toward the Bullsmobile. Mr. Bowman gave Dave a light punch on the arm. "Hey, I want to thank you for blowing the game open in the fourth quarter," he said. "Like I told you before, if it'd come down to a buzzer-beater, you guys would have sent me right back to the hospital."

"Come on, Mr. Bowman," Dave said, "don't even joke about that!"

Mr. Bowman took Dave's hand. "That was really nice, what you did in there with the trophy."

Dave just looked up at him, a little embarrassed.

"No, really," Mr. Bowman continued. "You've got to understand something. Ever since Mrs. Bowman passed away, Nate and you guys—and your basketball—that's been my life."

Dave nodded.

"All last week, while I was lying in my hospital bed, I thought about my son, Nate, coaching, and about you guys finally beating the Slashers and winning the championship. And you know what, Droopy?" he asked, gripping Dave's hand more tightly. "I think more than anything, that's what pulled me through."

About the Author

Hank Herman is a writer and newspaper columnist who lives in Connecticut with his wife, Carol, and their three sons, Matt, Greg, and Robby.

His column, The Home Team, appears in the *Westport News*. It's about kids, sports, and life in the suburbs.

Although Mr. Herman was formerly the editor-in-chief of *Health* magazine, he now writes mostly about sports. At one time, he was a tennis teacher, and he has also run the New York City Marathon. He coaches kids' basketball every winter and Little League baseball every spring.

He runs, bicycles, skis, kayaks, and plays tennis and basketball on a regular basis. Mr. Herman admits that he probably spends about as much time playing, coaching, and following sports as he does writing.

Of all sports, basketball is his favorite.